Elsie Tries a Triad

Written by Eileen Blake
Illustrated by Rachel Ivanyi

Elsie Tries a Triad created by Eileen Blake 2025

A project of FRU Publications, LLC

ISBN: 979-8-218-60214-7

First Edition

To my friends C. Austin, Trent, and Ivan whose support and
encouragement made this book possible.

And to Mike, who made everything possible.

This is Elsie

When it comes to hugs
and kisses,

Elsie likes Misters as well as Misses.

That's the way that she was born.
And that makes her a unicorn.

One fine day while at the gym,
Elsie ran right into Him.

Handsome, funny, and oh so smart,
Elsie looked and lost her heart.

So many things to talk about
and then one day he asked her out.

E lsie and Mister talked every day,
and after a while began to play.

"You are perfect!" Mister said.
But Elsie smiled and shook her head.

"No one is perfect, don't you see?
Not even a unicorn such as me.

Saying so is nice of you
but 'perfect' is hard to live up to."

After lots of hugs and kisses,
he introduced her to his Misses.

She was cute and smart as hell.
Elsie fell for her as well.

There were hugs and sighs and loving looks.
They talked about their favorite books.

They went to concerts and to plays.
Those were very happy days.

"Move in with us and we'll be three."
But Elsie didn't quite agree.

"Mister, Misses don't you see?
It always was and will always be,
the two of you and then just me.

What you have belongs to you,
the life you have is made for two.

If I don't fit into your home;
then I'll be left out on my own."

"Move in with us and share our home."
But Elsie said, "I need to roam.

I have a home and things to do.
I have a job, just like you."

Moving in was a great big deal.
She needed to know that this was real.

She loved them both very much
but sometimes they seemed out of touch.

"We'll build a nest," the couple said,
so we can sleep and play in bed."

Elsie agreed to move ahead,
but at a pace that worked for her,
something made her not quite sure.

Things were moving very fast.
Who knew how long this would last?

She would stay at her place for a while
and visit them as a trial.

If things went well then, she'd move in,
and their lives together would begin.

S o many things were going great,
but they told Elsie she had to wait.

For playtime she was good enough,
but not so much for other stuff.

If she agreed to improve herself,
they would take her off the shelf.

All she really had to do
was see things from their point of view.

If she would just fall in line,
then everything would be just fine.

Then one day, the last straw fell,
Mister and Misses had things to tell.

"We've made decisions on our own,
all about your future home."

"You'll live with us," Misses said,
"and sometimes you can share our bed."

Mister added "But you'll be living in our home,
so sometimes you will sleep alone."

They both told Elsie,
"There's no need to work and earn your pay,
you can cook and clean here all day."

This made Elsie feel bad, partly angry, mostly sad.

"What can I do to make you see?
I'm not just yours, I belong to me.

I have a good life of my own,
I don't want to work in someone's home."

This made Mister very mad.
He told Elsie she was bad.

He didn't like her attitude
and told her she lacked gratitude.

"It's our home and we know best;
you should be glad to share our nest."

"But surely, Misses you agree,
it's not wrong to be just me."

Misses flatly refused to see.
She told Elsie to let things be.

Elsie's protests went unheeded,
they told her just what she needed.

Tired of being told what to do,
she decided she was through.

The time had come that fateful day
to say goodbye and walk away.

21

Elsie's heart was full of wishes.
She would miss
the hugs and the kisses.

She would miss the talking and the laughter.

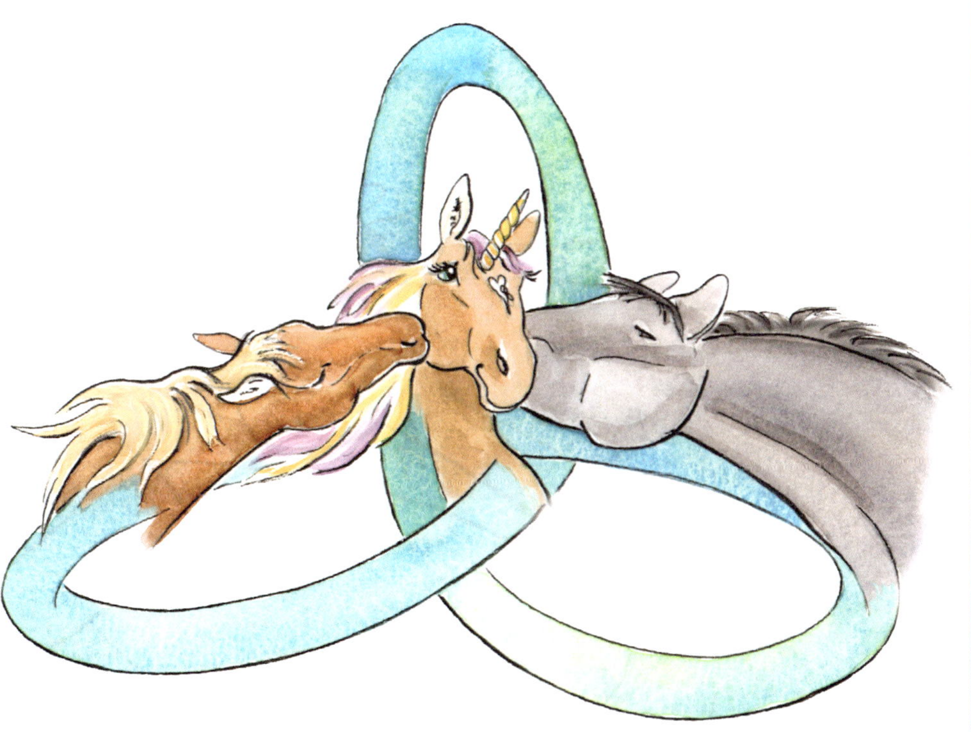

And the dreams of ever after.

E lsie settled in at home,
free to dream and free to roam.

As hard as leaving was to do,
she knew her values to be true.

Even though her heart was sore,
she knew that she deserved much more.

Time would mend her broken heart,
and she would make a brand-new start.

Mister and Misses expressed surprise.
Didn't Elsie realize?

How lucky she was to be their pet.
Just what was it she didn't get?

They had showered her with love and care.
Leaving them was so unfair.

They forgot if they ever knew
that unicorns are people too.